Summer's Winter

Summer's Winter

REBECCA KERR

FABLE
ARCHIVISTS

Author's Note

This story is an experimental exploration of the romantic comedy form. I set out to work with the "seven basic romantic comedy beats" as described by Billy Mernit in *Writing the Romantic Comedy*, while also subverting and playing with some familiar tropes.

Content Warning: Please note that the chapters written for Eddie contain explicit depictions of violence by a sociopathic vigilante and scenes of kidnapping by time-travelling highlanders. If you find these themes uncomfortable, feel free to skip those specific chapters called *Chapters for Eddie*.

Thank you for joining me on this creative journey. I hope you enjoy the blend of humour, experimentation, and heartfelt storytelling.

1

THE CHEMICAL EQUATION

Five people are seated, facing towards Kym. One is eagerly listening to every word, the others are playing on their phone and whispering to each other. Amongst them are eleven empty seats, all cramped into this unloved, uncoloured room. Kym is looking down, reading out loud from a book. Her book. She manages only quick glances as the lack of people deflates her self-esteem. Putting on a sense of extroversion, she takes it one word at a time.

After a few pages, Kym closes the book. With a deep breath of courage, she lifts her eyes to the people before her and manages to push her lips into a smile. If only it is a convincing one. The five people clap out of sync and with minimal effort.

Jeevika has been playing on her phone, just like the others. She looks up when the room goes silent and joins Kym. Her aura showing that she has some importance. In fact, she's Kym's publicist.

Jeevika says, "Thank you for that wonderful piece, Kym. If you enjoyed this little excerpt, Kym will be commencing signings in fifteen minutes. But we do have a few minutes for any burning questions."

No one puts their hand up, making Kym's stomach twist. Her palms are sweaty. She swallows. 'I chose the wrong career,' she thinks to herself.

"We hope to see you all shortly," Jeevika says, then makes her way to a nearby desk to prepare for Kym's signing.

A teenage girl with a sweet smile is waiting. The girl says, "Oh, wow, hi. I loved your book. I read it in a single night. I couldn't put it down. Wow. You're here. Signing books. I have a 1st edition and... will you sign it?"

Kym looks at her with a fake smile. She can't understand why this teenager is gushing so much. "I'm glad you enjoyed it. Who should I make it out to?"

"Beth. Oh wow. Thank you so much. I just loved your character Billy. He's my ideal guy. I hope to find a guy like that. I mean, there must be a perfect someone out there for everyone right? Did you base him on someone you know?"

"No," Kym says simply as she writes in the book.

"Oh. Okay. That's cool. I mean... He seems so real."

"I'm a writer," Kym says. "It's my job to make believable characters." Kym hands the now confused Beth her book.

"Thank you, I guess," Beth says then leaves.

"Pull it in, Kym," Jeevika warns under her breath.

The next eager young fan approaches. This time, with a friend who doesn't look as happy.

"Hi. Thank you for coming today. Are you enjoying Perth?" says the long, honey-haired girl with the toothy grin.

"I'm from Perth," Kym says, taking a book from Jeevika, and writes in it.

"Oops," the girl laughs. "My bad. Thank you for coming. Kate and I love your book. We've been debating about something."

"Did Billy, like, have a twisted thing for that goldfish," asks Kate, the girl with the snooty scowl.

"What?" Kym arches an eyebrow.

"You know that time he sat on the couch pouring his feelings out to the goldfish," Kate says.

Kym glances at Jeevika, begging to be saved. When she didn't bite, Kym says to the cranky girl, "No," and hands the book to Kate's friend.

Kym waits until the girls are far enough away before she says to Jeevika, "thanks for the save."

"You need to practice. I'll step in before things get too bad."

"Humph." Kym hates this part of writing. Getting out there and promoting her book. She is a proud introvert, preferring the solitary life. Which is why she chose writing as a career. And yet, here she is, front and centre at an event that requires her to talk to strangers.

"Would you like a coffee?" Jeevika asks, pulling Kym from her trance.

"Sure."

As Jeevika walks away, Kym gives out a frustrated breath. Of the five people who attended the reading, only two wanted their book signed. Trying to distract herself from falling into an abyss of self-doubt and depression, she pulls another book and signs it, getting it ready for the bookshelf.

Now is the perfect time to meet the protagonist, Kymberly Newman. She's a debut author promoting her first book on a small tour around Perth.

There is currently no room in the budget to be able to travel around the country to promote her book, so she settles for the five remaining notable bookstores in Perth. Well, more like 4.5 bookstores.

Her book, *Autumn's Spring*, is one of

those books that requires a certain niche market, that will not be named.

You know who you are.

A late-forty-something-year-old man walks over. Kym takes that deep breath, waiting for the number of ridiculous questions that men his age tend to give her.

"So, you wrote a book," he says picking up one of the copies and inspects the back cover. "Any good?"

Every inch of Kym's body wants to say some smart-ass reply but in the back of her mind she can hear the echoing screams of Jeevika telling her to be nice and sell a book.

"Well, that depends," she begins, "do you like stories written by a local author about a young girl who's looking for herself and decides to go on a road trip around Australia."

"I'm not sure if I'd be able to connect with the main character," he says, returning the book to the table.

"Yeah, well she's not the main character per se. There's one chapter that is told through the point of view of a goldfish."

"Why?"

"Why not?" she says.

They leer at each other as though preparing for war.

She huffs a breath. "Look, the story is about a road trip but is not about her but about the people she meets and impacts."

"Hmmm." He taps his fingers on the book. "And you're signing today?"

Kym bites her lip, nearly drawing blood. The urge to share her sarcastic thoughts is ready to explode. Thankfully, Jeevika is returning with her coffee.

'I'll show her just how delightful I can be,' Kym thinks.

"Sure am." Kym smiles.

"Hmmm," he mutters again. "Maybe my niece would like a signed book by some local."

'Some local?' Kym thinks with clenching her teeth.

"Would you like that personalised?" Jeevika asks, as though knowing Kym's reaching the point of no return.

"Nah. She'll be right," he says.

Kym takes one of the books and signs it 'To eBay, with love Kymberly Newman.' While a part of her knows it's wrong, she just couldn't help herself.

"So, I have some good news for you," Jeevika says with excitement. "You've been given a go ahead for a second book. They're giving you an advance of five thousand, but you have to have a completed manuscript by December."

"That's only three months away." The shock distracts Kym from the fact that she's just scored a second book deal.

"Well, they are aiming for a love story that has a Valentines release."

"A love story?"

"Well, they read *Autumn's Spring*, and they loved the triangle between Laura, Steven and Tania."

"There was no love triangle."

"Really. Are you sure?"

"I'm pretty sure."

"But there was that scene by the duck pond where Laura and Tania shared that moment before Steven stole Laura's heart," Jeevika says. Kym arches and eyebrow at her. "Kym. This is a second book deal. Authors very rarely get this chance so early in their career. If you don't want it, I can tell them no."

"Sure, why not?" Kym says with hesitating confidence. She takes a sip of hercoffee, burning her tongue. "It'll be a good challenge for me." She knows deep down; this won't end well.

As Kym walks back to her car, her phone sings. A soft smile pulls on her lips as she reads the name.

"Eddie, my wonderful editor," Kym says with a voice that is neither excited or annoyed. Maybe somewhere in between.

Kym decides to walk through the city to do some idle window shopping and speaking to her one-and-only editor. They both previously worked so well together on *Autumn's Spring* that she only trusts him look over her work.

"Jeevika has told me that you said yes to another book deal," Eddie says with his cheerful tune.

"Well, I did consider saying no," she says. She decides to sit down on a bench and people-watch while she chats. "Romance stories aren't really my thing."

"Well, it's the one genre that's gaining traction right now. And we need to compete with other big titles coming out."

"Big titles? They're having me compete against big titles?"

Eddie laughs. "Hey, it's a book deal. You've accepted, now let's make a book."

"Romance?"

"Yes, romance."

"I'm the last person who should be writing this."

"Kym, we want that wacky, weird, sarcastic humour of yours. Make it bad if you like. As long as it sells at Valentines."

"Do people still celebrate that?"

"Some do. Those looking for love."

Kym's body shivers at the word... Love. She remembers she once tried a relationship, in High School. She doesn't care for it much then and feels she won't so much now.

She observes a couple sitting at the cafe across from her. They seem happy. They don't look like they're tired of one another. They don't look in love either. She thinks that 'maybe they're just colleagues having lunch.'

Eddie breaks the silence and asks, "When can you have a summary and chapter sent to me?"

She releases a hard breath. "I don't know. It's so soon after this one. A month?"

"A week?" he replies.

"Twenty-eight days?"

"Seven days?"

She rolls her eyes and groans. "I can't just switch over. I'm a creative who needs time. I need inspiration to hit me."

"What about a change of scenery? There's some money in the budget."

"Ha. You're gonna pay for a trip for me?" her scepticism runs deep.

"I'm not. The company will. How about Paris?"

"You're pulling my leg, right?"

"A little. What about a place most writer's dream about? A cottage in the countryside. Somewhere in Scotland."

"Will you stop teasing me."

"Not teasing this time. The company has a deal with a bed and breakfast in Scotland. There's a room there that's always available. And don't worry, they'll pay for the airfares and food etc, you just need to keep the lights on here."

"Seriously?"

"Yes. Seriously."

The mere thought of Scotland sparks her interest. She remembers that the setting of a lot of those romance novels is set there.

Something about time travelling highlanders.

"Maybe it'll do," she says to Eddie. "I can write anything?"

"What are you thinking?"

"I'm thinking a cliche I don't have to think too hard about."

"No, you cannot do time travelling highlanders," Eddie says, reading her mind.

Kym hates it when Eddie does that. He seems to know exactly what she's thinking all the time. Which is why she feels he makes the best editor for her. He understands what she's trying to write.

"Stop doing that," she demands. "What kind of romance do you want?"

"Anything but that. The world has enough of it," he says, making her laugh.

"Is 'writer goes to Scotland and finds love' off limits?" she asks, half expecting him to say no.

He stays silent for a moment. "Sounds a bit too similar to your current one."

"I thought you were gonna say cliche,"

she says. "But instead, you join the others in thinking my current book is a romance."

"I know it's not, but many perceive it as a light romance," he says. "Make it feel different enough and I'd say go for it."

"It wasn't a romance," Kym growls, startling the person beside her. She readjusts herself then drops the volume of her voice. "I'll write their stupid romance. Then people will see *Autumn's Spring* is not a romance."

Eddie chuckles. "Let me know when you'd like to go, and I'll organise it."

"How about today?" she says, hoping to get out of this book tour.

"It'll take me at least two days to organise. Start getting everything ready and I'll give you a call tomorrow."

"What about my book tour," she asks, praying that he agrees it's over.

"Jeevika won't be happy."

"Leave Jeevika to me," he says. "I want your creative spark to switch gears. Also, I'm being serious that I want a summary and first chapter this time next week."

"Sure," she says. "I'll chat to you later."

"Later, Kym."

Kym puts her phone in her pocket and continues watching the couple at the cafe. She doesn't care how creepy she looks. To her, this was research.

They both wore professional clothing. Him a grey suit. Her a white blouse tucked into a pencil skirt. Both groomed well. Clearly on a high wage bracket. They drink their coffee gently. They eat their healthy food eloquently.

Once they've finished, he looks at his watch. They both smile with a touch of sadness. Before they leave, they share a rather intimate kiss.

"So, not colleagues?" Kym says to herself, almost like it was a question rather than a statement.

Kym groans to herself. The thought of stooping to writing a romance pains her. But she cannot pass a second book deal so soon. After all, she's gotta pay the bills.

2

MEET CUTE

Within the week, Kym finds herself in Scotland, driving towards the B&B in a cute little taxi. They travel down an empty road surrounded by a sublime landscape. The colossal mountains are a stark contrast to her city back home.

Breathing in the fresh air, Kym absorbs the sunlight that glitters off the nearby loch. "Wow, this is beautiful," she says.

"That it is lass," the driver says. "This is a bonny place. We get young writers such as yerself out here every Autumn. No one famous, though."

Kym makes a sound that's a mixture of humour and disappointment. She can't help but think he's just purposely insulted her.

As they pass through a small village, Kym takes everything in. Close to the side of the main road, there's a few small stores.

One in particular stands out to her. An old-fashioned bookstore, with white-panelled wall and a dark-brown roof. She makes a mental note to come and see the store once she's settled.

Only a few people are walking the streets. Their leering eyes follow the taxi. She can't help but wonder if she's become a much-needed topic for gossip here.

They approach the two-story, stone cottage situated in a meadow, close to the loch. Smoke billows from the chimney. Its green roof almost blending into the scenery. A sign, with B&B inscribed, is embedded in the stone wall.

Once he stops. The driver says, "We're here, lass."

"Thank you," she says in return and exits the taxi. She pays the driver, takes her belongings, says goodbye and enters the B&B.

The door creaks open and she steps into a small foyer. The soft fragrance of rose compliments the smoky wood fire, crackling in the parlour. An unattended reception desk is in the back left corner, covered in flyers of local sites to visit. In the other corner, there's a place to hang coats, and currently, there's only one dark blue coat.

"Ye must be Kymberly?" says a woman coming down the stairs.

"I am," Kym replies. She approaches the counter, with bags at her side.

"Ye must be tired, lass," the woman says. "I've just finished preparing yer room. Follow me. I'm Maggie."

"This place is stunning," Kym says as she follows.

"Why, thank ye, dear."

Kym's room is at the end of the hall. It's a cosy room with a kitchenette for making tea. There's a small table with two wooden chairs, housing well-kept burgundy cushions. On the table, there's a small pot plant, a ponytail palm to be precise. The double bed is at the back, next to the large window. And to the right, a door leads to a private shower and toilet.

"I can have a light lunch ready at twelve thirty for ye," Maggie says. Which was about twenty minutes from now. Kym's starving and could eat her own arm if she has to wait any longer.

The first thing that Kym does is have a shower and put on some fresh clothes. Drying her hair, she looks over the ponytail plant and notices the card.

I hope you like the room. Relax and send me chapters asap. – Eddie

Kym smiles as she brushes her fingers along the thin leaves of the palm. The quiet brings her comfort, finally giving her the escape from humanity that she's been craving since her book tour started.

Tossing the towel over one of the chairs, Kym explores the rest of the room until she makes her way to the window. She tugs open the latch and takes in the crisp, cool breeze that rolls over the loch. She takes in the earthy fragrance while contemplating the view.

With the five minutes before lunch, she takes out her coffee-stained notepad to start taking notes for the chapter for Eddie.

On the flight over, Kym watched a film about a serial killer. While watching, she wondered how the story would have turned out if it was written like a rom-com. And, from the point of view of a serial killer.

Kym gets so caught up in the idea that she completely misses when Maggie delivers a sandwich and juice to her room. Maggie appears unaffected, as though this is something she experiences regularly.

The moment Kym finishes the chapter she emails it to Eddie.

From the moment Kym passed the bookshop earlier in the day, it's like it's been begging for her to enter and browse the shelves. Maybe find something that could help her find inspiration for her thriller romance.

After sending the email to Eddie, Kym walks to the village, about a fifteen-minute trip, to check out the bookshop. Peering through the frosted glass of the door, she takes a deep breath, gripping the handle tightly. The bells chime as she pushes through.

At the far end of the shop, a head pops up from behind a bookshelf. The sixty-something-year-old woman has eyes brighter than a twenty-year-old and her dimpled smile shows a decent set of veneered teeth.

"Hiya. Lemme know if ya need any help." Her thick American accent is a stark contrast to this little Scottish bookstore. And, as quick as her head pops up, it was gone again.

"Thank... Thank you," Kym stutters.

Kym takes her time browsing the store. Her fingers dance across the spines, jumping between new titles and old. Occasionally, she picks up a book and reads the blurb. Nothing seems to grab her interest.

"Did ya need some help there?" says the head that once again pops up. "Ya sure look like ya do."

The sixty something year-old woman emerges completely. Her clothing immediately stands out. A loose-fitting Metallica T-shirt draping over her tight, torn jeans and slender body. Her silver hair is being kept in that short pixie style, with hooped earrings nearly touching her shoulders. The woman bounces her way towards Kym.

"Ya look like ya're searchin' for the perfect book," she says with determination. "Lemme see..." She looks Kym up and down, while making that hmmmm sound. Kym arches an eyebrow. "Single gal from outta town tryin' to get away from it all, huh?" Kym stares dumbfounded as the woman takes off to the back of the shop. "I think I have just the book for ya," she yells out.

Kym continues looking through the bookshelves. There must be over a thousand of books, but she's either suffering from choice paralysis or jetlag. Each time the cover art sparks her interest, the blurb puts her off.

"I just got half a dozen of these sent to me by mistake," the woman calls as she returns. "Was gonna put them on the shelf this afternoon. Here ya go."

Kym takes the book and with one glance at the cover she scoffs. 'Am I really that obviously sad and predictable?' she thinks to herself. The book is *Autumn's Spring.*

"I read it last night. Ya know, it's a real good read. Light and quick. Perfect for us single lady types. And lemme tell ya about this four-way, square-shaped thing goin' on with the main character and these three guys."

"What, no there isn't," Kym says in that immediate defensive tone. "It was only ever Steven that she had a thing for."

"Ah, so ya've read it?" The woman's eyes light up. "See, I would argue that Davey and Scott were both chasin' after her too, and between you and me, I'm pretty sure Laura and Davey got together that night after the meat tastin' ceremony."

"What on earth gave you that idea?" All niceties are gone. This woman has unknowingly declared war. "Laura didn't even like Davey. He was responsible for her being expelled from the girls against home-bred chickens club. That was her life. She despised him for that."

"Pfft. That was just him getting her to grow up and move forward. He loved her that much that he got her to leave that ridiculous club behind and follow her passions. And for that she was grateful. Hence the 'special night.' The name's Jill by the way," she says with a smile.

Kym stares blankly, contemplating about Jill's theory. "But..."

Jill's grin overtakes her wrinkled face.

"No. He was..." Kym hesitates.

Jill nods slowly, trying to encourage Kym to follow.

"Huh." Kym has to admit it was a good

theory. "I never really thought about it that way before."

"Yeah, that writer really knew what she was doing," Jill said

"Clearly she didn't," Kym mumbles to herself.

"I mean, it takes a real creative mind to put a beehive in a lighthouse, stick it in a desert, and make it work," Jill says. "So did you like it?"

Kym clears her throat, "I think I'd be a little biased."

"Resemble your life a little bit too much?" Jill says with that sympathetic tone as she touches Kym's elbow. Kym holds back the urge to swing at the sixty-some-thing-year-old lady with the American ac-cent who calls herself Jill.

"Well, I wrote it," Kym says as she hands the book back.

Jill sizes Kym up, then smiles. She takes the book from her, opens the back cover, and holds it up. Eyes darting between Kym and what Kym knows to be her portrait. Jill squints her eyes. 'Yeah, yeah, it's only six months old,' Kym thinks to herself.

"So, you didn't really see the Laura and Davey thing when you were writing? Or the flirting between Laura and Scott at Donna's poodle's third birthday?" Jill says.

"What?" Kym continues her confusion.

"Would ya sign the books that I got in?" Jill asks with that sweet, innocent 'please help me make money' smile. Kym is immediately reminded of Jeevika's passion for reaching those KPIs.

"Sure," Kym replies.

Jill's eyes brighten. She hands the book back to Kym and quickly runs for the back room. "Make a start on that one and I'll get the others," Jill yells out. "Thanks so much for this."

Diving into her boring, black bag, Kym gets tangled up while searching for a pen. With a fire of frustration, Kym rips her bag from her shoulder, the swinging movement smacks against the bookshelf beside her. Books flump onto the floor, oozing like a liquid at her feet. With a deep sigh, she flings the bag back onto her shoulder, knocking over more books. She stills herself, rubbing a hand all over her face. Groaning.

Clearing her throat, she picks her pen from the floor and proceeded to write an entry into the book. The utter mess of books will have to wait. This was going to be a great entry. Something that will change the life of someone. To inspire them to follow their dreams.

Kym pauses, staring blankly at the pen. 'If only it could write for me,' she thinks to herself.

Kym flicks to Chapter 4, and then as though by sheer willpower, the pen began to write for her.

"Hello," says a Scottish man's voice. "D'ye need some help?"

"No, I'm okay," Kym replies, her eyes glued to the page, captivated by her own words.

"Ye sure about that?" says the voice.

A very frustrated Kym takes her eyes from the page and moves them to the thirty-something-year-old man, a little taller than her, in a police uniform. His Arabic coffee, most likely the Catuia variety, coloured eyes stare curiously at her. The rest of his face, however, gives off that impatient vibe that says he would rather be somewhere else and yet here he is talking to her. Regardless of the man's attitude though, Kym still has a soft spot for a man in a uniform. Especially a police uniform. It was probably due to one of those midday films her mum watched when she was a kid.

"I'm sure," she says.

"And what d'ye think ye're doing to the shop?" he asks, pointing at the mess that she's just made. "Why ye're vandalising the books?"

An amused sound emerges from Kym. He raises an eyebrow.

"This isn't what it looks like," Kym says in defence. "This was an accident. That I was going to fix. After I finished writing in the book... Yeah, that sounds worse than it is. You see I'm actually the author of this book, and the owner of the store asked if I could sign it."

The officer stares at Kym without a speck of emotion. After a rather awkward, long pause, he pulls out a notebook and begins writing in it.

"Uh, what are you doing?" Kym asks.

"Taking notes. I can see this is gonna be a rough report," he says.

"I'm sorry, what? What report? I knocked a couple of books down and signed a book that I wrote. As asked by the owner of the store." Kym looks to his name bade thinking maybe a little human connection will help smooth things over. "Hi, Officer Campbell, I know this may sound a little weird, but I assure you I am telling you the truth."

"Ye know this isn't the first time I've heard this story from tourists."

"Really?" Kym asks a little stunned. "People use that as an excuse to vandalise a small village bookstore?"

The two lock eyes in a standoff.

"Now, are ye gonna tell me the real story?" He returns to his notepad.

"I'm telling you the real story."

"I found them!" Jill screams from the back room as she shuffles her way to us. "Malcolm. What brings ya into my shop today? You chasing your next winter read?"

"Afternoon, Jill," he says, his tone softening slightly. "Saw a bit of commotion from outside."

"Commotion?" Jill looks around and sees the books all over the floor.

"Yeah... sorry about that," Kym says sheepishly. She hands Jill the signed book. "There was a fight between me and my bag. And the books were collateral damage."

"All in the line of duty," Jill says and starts cleaning up.

When Kym begins to assist, Jill pushes the five other books into her hands.

"I'll clean up the mess. You can sign these," Jill says, returning to the mess.

Malcolm returns his notebook to his pocket and gives Kym the once-over, still without a speck of emotion.

"Would you like to buy a signed copy of my book?" Kym says with that sarcastic tone that says, 'Take that mister.'

"Sorry to disturb ye both. Enjoy yer afternoon," Malcolm says as he walks casually towards the exit.

"It was nice seeing ya, Malcolm," Jill calls out after him. Once he's back on the street, she continues, "Such a sweet man. I'm completely dumbfounded that he's still single. If I was twenty years younger, I'd swipe him up without a second thought."

3

CHAPTER FOR EDDIE

LAVENDER

A sparkling field of dew rested on blades of grass. Bare feet left footprints as the jewels were buried into the earth. The chill in the air begged me to put on a jacket or, at the very least, some shoes. But I only wore a thin cloth shirt that draped to my knees. A pile of clothes waited on a rock nearby.

Croaking frogs competed with the crickets. The occasional splash would come from the fish-eating bugs that skipped on the surface. At the edge of the riverbank, I dipped my toes. Deep breath.

"You must be Sam," said a gruff voice.

He was a lot taller than me. Taller than he said he was. Hmm. That's never happened before.

"Calvin?"

"Yeah." He stepped closer.

"I don't see the rope I asked for."

"It's in my car."

Rolling my eyes, my attention returned to the water. I stepped in. Why do some of them always try to get me to their car? Is it a safety net for them?

"Fine," he growled and stormed off.

The bottom of my shirt gently swam against the current. It was about ten minutes before he returned. Which meant he parked further away than I'd hoped.

"I've got your rope." He threw it on the riverbank.

"You did agree to be here, right? I told you I liked rope."

"Just... Don't tie it too tight."

I reached out and grabbed it. The feel of the hard plastic made my stomach turn. Even though I'd ask for natural twine, most of them always brought the artificial kind.

He released a hard breath before stripping down and joining me. I pressed his back against the bark of a tree and bound his hands together.

"You better be a good fuck," he groaned.

I locked eyes with him. "Who said we were having sex?"

He curled his brows. "What?"

"I said I would liberate you."

It was just bright enough to see him turn pale.

"This isn't funny." He struggled against the rope.

"I don't know who you killed in that moment of passion last week. A friend? A family member? A lover? And really, I don't care. What I do care about is that you used my name to cover up your crime."

The whites of his eyes grew as he sucked in air. "Wait. This is a joke, right? You're role playing? I didn't agree to this."

While he struggled, I drew my athame from the clay bank. He struggled. The water washed mud from the blade. He struggled.

"I find if you just accept it, it's more peaceful."

"What the fuck? Get the fuck away from

me," he screamed.

The cold metal pressed just above his navel. His lip trembled. The blade slid over flesh. Trapped blood now flowed, dripping into the river. Shock stole his screams. With more pressure, splashes threw bloodied water over my shirt. His whole body shook as his insides now fed the tadpoles.

"It's okay," I said. "It'll be over shortly."

It wouldn't take long for him to stop breathing. As the blood left his veins, a cold blanket would envelop him. A cold that I was more than used to feeling. It followed me everywhere. But now, I was accustomed to it.

He gurgled and choked.

I held my ear to his mouth. "Is there something after? I don't know. I don't think so."

As the light in his eyes faded, Theo flashed in front of me. I could only imagine what he was thinking right now. Was he at home sound asleep, without a care? Was he scrolling through news feeds looking at this arsehole's work? Thinking it was me?

I dug my toes into the muddy earth. I stepped closer. The athame now an extension of my rage. I struck the blade into his heart. Twisted. Blade across his throat.

"You fucking made me and my best-friend fight you arsehole," I screamed, inches from his face.

Blood drooled. Blank stare. Gurgled reflex. His light was gone. He'd been liberated.

4

SEXY COMPLICATION

Kym's been in this little town for several days now. She's become friendly with Maggie, from the B&B, Jill from the bookshop, and Greg from the grocery store. She made a connection with Greg when he noticed Kym's daily venture for junk food. It was on day three that their daily conversations start up. Greg was a forty-something-year-old man, with dark brown hair and a short, trimmed beard with orange splashed throughout.

She's seen Malcolm around the village a couple of times. Sometimes the both of them share a glance. A smile pulls at her lips each time she spies him. Her little triumph at the bookstore when she got a little 'told you so' moment will bring her a little buzz for the rest of her life.

After buying her daily supply of junk food

from the shop, Kym gets into her little hire car. Kym has decided to go visit a local lighthouse for a little inspiration while writing. As the weather is a little... well... cold, light rain, she has decided to just stay in the car when she gets there and enjoy the view. And, before she can drive off, and as though fate plays a part, her phone rings. It's Eddie. She puts the phone on the holder, plugs it in and answers it.

"Hey Eddie," she says, starting the car.

"Hey. How are you goin? Wait, are you driving? Should you be driving while talking to me?"

"It's fine," she says, pulling out of the car park.

There's a storm rolling in and she is desperate to get to the lighthouse and back to the B&B before it starts raining. She's looking forward to locking herself up in the B&B, sitting next to the fire and reading a book.

"So, how was the chapter I sent?" she asks.

"It was... a draft, I guess." He takes a pause that Kym barely notices. "Uh... how's the other chapters?"

"Uh... Okay, I guess," she mocks his uneasiness.

"Look, I'm gonna be honest. That chapter... I think you should give it another shot."

Kym's brows touch each other. "What's wrong with it?"

"You're meant to be writing a light romance, not a psychological thriller on steroids."

"What? I'm setting up the world and the characters." Kym slams on her brakes when a car comes out of nowhere. The wheels skid a little, but she manages to stop in time. The other driver doesn't even notice how close they've come to a debt to the local mechanic, Geoff. She hopes that Eddie didn't hear the little event.

"I heard that," he growls. "Pull the car over."

"Okay, okay," Kym lies. She continues driving, but this time, a little more cautiously.

"I need you to send me a new chapter, this time not so dark. It's okay to have a murder mystery but preferably don't have the main character be a sociopath."

"So, you hate it?" Kym says.

"I think you can do better."

"Which is a polite way of saying you hate it." If she didn't have to keep her hands on the wheel, she'd rub her face. "When do you want it?"

"As soon as you can."

She grips the wheel and shakes it. It's stiff plastic unaffected by her temper tantrum. "Fine."

A light rain taps on the windscreen. Small puddles on the side of the road dance with each drop. Even in this cold, wet weather, the scenery is absolutely stunning. She could stay here forever; she thinks to herself. Maybe she could just become a detective who solves crimes out in the countryside. The token Aussie who comes and changes the town with her Aussie slang and charm. Maybe she could boss Malcolm around.

"Look, I didn't hate it, per se. It's just different than what the powers that be are expecting. Keep that idea for another book.

Just... not this one, okay?"

"Eddie," she says in a long whine that lasts a few seconds. "Romance is not my thing."

"Kym, you already have an advance. They're paying for you to be there. You've signed a contract." Eddie has moved away from his light, almost geek girl, vocals and becomes the growling editor who is reaching the end of his thread with the super, stubborn creative.

"I know. I know. What do you want me to write? Tell me and I'll write it."

"Write a romance. A light, fluffy, fun romance that has a little of that quirk of yours."

There's a tight knot in Kym's stomach. "How do I write about something I know nothing about?"

Kym can hear her digital clock tick, that is if it could make that ticking sound. But she imagines that it would have a little twang to it as it moved from a three to a four.

Eddie is a little too silent for a little too long and Kym is starting to become more nervous. "Eddie? You still there?"

"Yes." She imagines that he's pinching the bridge of his nose. Eyes closed tight. Focusing on his breaths. "Write a sequel for *Autumn's Spring*. Call it Summer's Winter."

"But that story is over."

"Follow Laura's next road trip. Maybe set it there, in Scotland."

She stares out the window. "Maybe that could work." She actually wasn't sure it would work. When she finished writing *Autumn's Spring*, she imagined that Laura did a Thelma and Louise style exit. An idea sparks and Kym wonders if she can write her as a ghost. She isn't going to tell Eddie until she sends through the new book summary and character sketches.

"I'll give it a go," she says.

"Thank you. Can you get them to me tonight? Just needs to be a rough idea."

"Uh, I'm not sure if I'll have reception tonight. There's a big storm coming."

He releases another hard breath. "Can you send them as soon as you can please?"

"Will do." She now wants the conversation

over, so she has time to get to the lighthouse and write his chapter. "See ya, Eddie."

"Sorry to be harsh, but I know you can do better."

"See ya, Eddie," she repeats.

"Oh, Kym, Laura cannot be a ghost."

"Get out of my head, you witch," Kym snaps.

Eddie snorts. "I'll call you tomorrow."

She ends the call. She doesn't want to hear his disappointed tone any longer. She needs to focus on the storm now. On getting back to that cosy little B&B.

The rain is heavy against the countryside, with the visibility being around ten metres. Kym's still decompressing after the call with Eddie, and she's finding it rather hard to navigate in this weather.

"Shit. I can't see a thing," she mumbles to herself as she wipes the fog from the windscreen.

The window wipers are thrashing back and forth, but they're useless. The rain slamming against the roof creates a deafening thunder. Echoes of a beeping tone leak through the chaos. Glancing at her phone again she finds that there's still no GPS connection.

"Connect. Please connect," Kym pleads.

A few meters up Kym notices water stretching the width of the road. In this slightly anxiety-fuelled moment, she estimates that the water level is shallow so she's unconcerned with possible complications occurring. So, she decides to ignore any potential issues.

Keeping her speed, she travels through, causing water to spray up the sides of the car. Her hands tighten around the steering wheel as she realises that the puddle was in fact deeper than predicted and now she's losing control of the car.

Thankfully, she manages enough control to steer off the road before her car comes to a stop. All by itself. This does not look good.

Disbelief fills her core.

"Don't! You! Dare!" Kym says through gritted teeth.

Attempting to start the car again was no

use. While the engine does turn over, it will not ignite. The car is dead.

"You. Gods. Damn. Piece. Of..."

Kym slams her hands against the steering wheel several times, ending with her banging her head against her seat. Then the steering wheel.

She checks her phone again.

No connection.

"Really?"

The water slamming against the metal of the car drives her to the edge. She taps her head against the steering wheel and contemplates whether crying would help the situation or not. But instead, she decides to use this moment to nap.

A really annoying tapping on the window wakes Kym from her nap. She glances at her phone to see that an hour has passed, and a quick glance out the windscreen shows that the rain is still just as thick.

The tapping starts up again. A rather disorientated Kym looks out the window next to her. The window beside her is completely fogged, but she can make out a yellow reflective strip.

"Please don't be Malcolm. Please. Don't. Be..." Kym whispers as she winds down the window.

It is, in fact, Malcolm, wearing his hi-vis uniform. Kym looks away instantly, trying to avoid looking at him, but she cannot help herself and steals quick glances.

"Are ye alright?" Malcolm asks.

"Umm. Well. Kinda." Kym begins to babble. "Embarrassing really. I drove through that puddle and, well, now she's not moving."

Malcolm looks back to the puddle, then back at Kym with a soft smile in his eyes. "Didn't ye slow down for it?" he asks.

"Well, Officer Campbell, clearly I didn't do the smart thing," Kym replies rudely. She looks away in disbelief. "Sorry. I've been sitting here with no phone signal for about an hour. Waiting for the rain to stop."

The pounding of the water and ice-cold wind reminds them both just how awkward this moment of silence is. After what felt like an eternity of hellish shame for Kym, Malcolm nervously clears his throat.

"Well come on. I'll take ye back to yers," Malcolm says with a little fear in his voice, that only a trained professional can pick up. "I mean, I'll give ye a lift home. You know. All part of the duty. Of being a police officer. Cause that's what I am. A police officer." Malcolm stands upright and winces at his words.

Kym has no idea how to respond to his behaviour, so instead thinks about his offer. More than anything, she's afraid to move out of this seat while a man in uniform was so close to her. Then there was the near possibility of her being in his car. She is bound to start some random babbling fit in his car. Then he'll easily guess her thing with uniforms.

Malcolm opens the door, making the decision for her.

"Come on," he says calmly while handing her a hi-vis waterproof jacket.

Kym's heart races in excitement. Her

dreams have come true. She does not hesitate from taking the jacket, putting it on, and basking in the fact that she is wearing an officer's jacket.

Kym grabs her keys and tosses them into the laptop bag. She clutches the bag under the jacket and once she is out of the car, Malcolm remains the perfect gentleman and closes the door behind her. He then proceeds to point her towards his car. Kym focuses on her breaths as they walked to his car. The only thoughts going through her mind, 'Just twenty steps to the car. Nineteen. Eighteen. Wait. Why am I counting steps? Stop counting steps.'

Malcolm first helps Kym into his car, then runs around to his side. Once inside he focuses on getting them both warm with the car's heater.

"I'm sorry," Kym says through chattering teeth, "I've messed your car up."

"It's just a wee bit of water. Worse things have happened to it," he replies with that Malcolm winning smile.

He awkwardly takes his soaked jacket off, throwing it into the back seat. As he does Kym begins searching her laptop bag. Mainly to distract herself from the officer stripping off his clothes next to her.

"Shit, shit, shit," Kym says, slamming her head on the headrest. She looks at Malcolm sheepishly, "Sorry. I don't usually swear so much."

"Ye okay?" he asks, concerned.

An embarrassed smile forms on Kym's lips, "I left my phone in the car."

There is an awkward moment of silence between the two before Kym decides to go back for her phone. Just as Kym opens the door, Malcolm leans over to close it. Holding her breath, Kym leans back as far as she can from him. She's a little confused about how she enjoyed the smell of him. She wonders what kind of aftershave that is.

"Dinnae be daft," Malcolm says as his eyes lock onto her.

The close proximity causes him to swallow hard. He quickly leans back into his seat and clears his throat.

"Ma house is..." he begins but pauses to clear his throat. "Ma house is just down the road. We can dry off and come back once the storm settles. Yer phone'll be safe."

Kym takes in the now raging storm. 'It can't be safe to keep driving,' she thinks, before saying it out loud.

"Is it safe to keep driving?" Kym asks.

"Nae. But we could make it to ma house. It's about a kilometre from here. We'll just take our time."

"Okay," Kym eventually replied.

"Right." Malcolm looks a little surprised. "Off we go then." He was becoming more nervous as he started the car. "Are ye comfortable? Feel free to take your jacket off and throw it in the back. We'll be at ma house in about five minutes. Unless we need to stop again. Then it might take longer. Maybe ye should keep the jacket on. To keep warm." It appears that Malcolm was starting to catch the babbling thing that Kym suffers from in nerve-racking situations.

As Malcolm drives off, Kym keeps trying to distract herself from the situation.

"Are ye warm enough?" Malcolm asked, "I can turn up the heat for ye." He begins messing with the dials. Bringing a smile to her frozen lips.

As they arrive at Malcolm's place, the storm has intensified. Clutching the laptop bag, Kym prepares to jump out of the car and make a run to the front door. The moment the car comes to a stop, Malcolm snatches the laptop from her and puts it in the backseat.

"Dinnae risk it. It'll be here after the storm," he says. "Come on."

He exits the car and Kym follows. On their dash to the front door, Malcolm makes the error of touching Kym's arm to guide her around a giant puddle. It's not that this touch wasn't unwelcome, it's that Kym wasn't expecting to feel something, like warmth, when he did.

Even though Kym had hoped she might have recovered from her stumbling reaction, except Malcolm tries to help steady her. As he touches her again, Kym's nerves cause her to react, thus taking Malcolm with her as they fall into the large puddle in his front yard.

The two find themselves waist-deep in icy water, the rain pounds hard on them. Both are shocked by the cold and take a moment to process what has just happened. Malcolm is the first to snap out of it as his attention quickly moves to Kym's wellbeing.

"Are ye okay?" he shouts through the deafening storm.

As soon as Kym responds with a nod Malcolm is on his feet and pulling Kym up with him. His firm gentle hold continues to direct Kym to his front door. The onset of hypothermia makes her immune to his touch this time.

As Malcolm puts his attention into unlocking the door, Kym steals quick glances of the man in uniform. Once inside, Malcolm immediately guides Kym to the bathroom.

"I'll get ye something warm to wear," Malcolm says then leaves her.

Kym closes the door and strips each of the soaked layers off. She waits in her tank top and thermal pants for Malcolm to return. The wet fabric clings tight to her, almost acting like a warm second skin. She takes this moment to look through Malcolm's things.

Next to the sink, she spies his toothbrush, the bamboo handle kind. She picks up his aftershave and smells it. It's called Earthy Spice. She has no idea what that means, but she does enjoy the scent of it. Her eyes close and images of Malcolm fill her mind. She is tempted to put a little on her wrists, but the tap on the door saves her from doing something that might be quite embarrassing.

Kym opens the door, half hiding behind it. He's still in his wet uniform. A wet uniform clinging to his body. He is still wearing his belt with cuffs and a taser. Kym notices his glance towards the mirror. His face turns pink. He then hands her the clothes and takes off.

She closes the door with a smirk and slips off the thermal pants. The new warm layers smelt like Malcolm. To her, it was like being hugged by him. Which was weird and makes her think about her life's priorities.

She hangs her clothes over racks, then ventures throughout the house to find Malcolm. She finds him in the kitchen putting on a dishwasher. She raises an eyebrow as she swears that she can smell sour milk in the air.

"Would ye like tea?" Malcolm asks.

"Sure," she says. "Black, please." She never had black tea. But she also didn't trust his milk right now.

Malcolm puts on the kettle on the stove and stands awkwardly in the kitchen corner. He couldn't possibly get any further away from her in this small space.

Kym looks him up and down. Eyebrow still raised. He was still soaked head to toe. She asks, "Aren't you cold?"

As though only just realising, he glances down in shock then takes off to his room.

Curiosity gets the better of Kym and she explores the next room. There are plants around the lounge room. A couch and chair.

A small coffee table. It is like most lounge rooms she has seen really. But more plants.

She approaches a bookcase and looks through the books. Most of them have over-the-top cracked spines. A range of mystery, adventure and romance. The romance books made her smile. She picks one up, called Romance in the Highlands. It is one of the books with a cracked spine and well-worn edges. She flicks through, then reads the blurb on the back. The book is about time-travelling highlanders, but this time, it was a female warrior coming to the present to grab a man and take him back in time. She scoffs, immediately thinking of Eddie. If Malcolm reads this stuff, then clearly she can write her novel on this topic, meaning Eddie was wrong.

As she stands here, looking at the book, she's getting ideas on how to approach the story. Following Eddie's suggestion, a sequel to *Autumn's Spring*, follows Laura on her new adventure in the past. 'Who wouldn't want to read it,' she thinks to herself.

Malcolm returns to the kitchen.

"Kym?" he calls out.

"Yeah?" she replies as she quickly places the book back.

Malcolm comes into the room and b-lines it to the chair near the window. He grabs something and shoves it behind some cushions and sits down. She raises an eyebrow, unsure how to take his reaction. Clearly, he's hiding something from her, something more embarrassing than books about time-travelling highlanders. She gives him the benefit of the doubt and not call him on it.

Now that Malcolm isn't wearing his uniform, she can think straight. Which involves noticing just how odd he is. He's sitting up straight on the edge of his chair, wringing his hands. She can't help but wonder if he really thinks she didn't notice his actions.

The kettle starts whistling. Malcolm is still hesitant to move. She raises an eyebrow and smirks at him.

"Would you like me to get that?" she asks.

"Nae," he says then heads for the kitchen.

Her eyes follow him for only a moment, then she goes immediately to his chair.

"How do ye have it?" Malcolm calls. "The tea. How do ye have yer tea?"

"Black," she says. Knowingly repeating herself.

Realising she has only seconds, she dives for the cushions. Her hands take hold of a hard rectangular object. She pulls it out. Her heart stops. It's her book. A copy of her book. There were sticky tabs throughout. She opens the book at one of the tabs. He's underlined a quote.

"And why would you think goldfish have no feelings? Is it because acknowledging their sentience threatens your precious agency?" Laura spits at Davey.

She hears movement from the kitchen. She immediately shoves the book back and returns to stand at the bookcase. She grabs a book from the shelf and uses it as a distraction. It's called *Me with You in the Outback.*

Malcolm appears with two cups of tea and hands one to Kym. His eyes drop to the book in her hands. His cheeks turn to a shade of magenta.

"Do you mind if I sit?" Kym asks as she puts the book back.

Malcolm's eyes are wide as he nods and points to the lounge. He sits on the chair hiding her book and sips his tea. He looks to the fireplace and moves to light it. He fumbles with lighting it, as though he's never done it before.

Kym holds the warm cup of aromatic tea in her hands. She watches the oddly behaving man in front of her. Malcolm has always been so confident and serious around Kym. But now, he appears affected by the cold. She considers calling an ambulance for him.

"Is everything okay?" Kym asks.

"Aye," he says simply. He strikes a flame and aims for loose threads of wood.

Kym looks around the room. She tries to understand this man a little more but finds it hard to put all the pieces together.

The two of them ended up having light conversations for the next few hours. She manages to get him talking about his book collection. Slowly, he reveals that he had a wife, who died four years ago. The romance books belonged to her, but he's read them since her death to feel some kind of connection to her.

Malcolm tells Kym that he knows he has to move on, meet new people, maybe have another relationship, but he feels awkward about it. Even as he talks about these feelings, his hands move nervously around his legs.

She ends up spending the nights in his guest room. It was a nice, cosy room and looked like some elderly lady furnished it. A handmade, floral quilt covers the double sized bed. Four pillows are packed against the wooden headboard. And the gentle scent of lavender helps her fall asleep.

5

THE HOOK

The sun is shining. Birds are singing. The garden is soaked from the rain the night before. Malcolm walks Kym up to the front door of the B&B. Kym is still wearing Malcolm's sweats and holding a bag with her now-dry clothes. She could have changed back into her clothes, but for some weird reason, she still wants to have Malcolm's clothes against her skin. Malcolm's back in uniform, making Kym's knees weak once again. But she has started to feel like she's building up an immunity the more she sees him. The more she's close to him.

It isn't long until they both spy Maggie peering through the dining window. Kym gives her a little wave. Maggie smirks, then drops the lace curtain in front of her eyes. But Maggie is clearly still watching.

"Well, thank you for letting me crash at

yours," Kym says. "And for the clothes...
And breakfast."

Kym begins to feel uncomfortable in the
silence. Malcolm hasn't spoken since they left
the car, which stands about ten meters away.
'Maybe I should cut him some slack,' she
thinks to herself. She looks around and spies
Maggie once again. This time, Betty is peering
next to her.

Kym says, "You know. We can always
give those old bats something juicy to talk
about."

Malcolm looks at her confused. Kym
makes sure that the women are watching as
she leans in and kisses Malcolm on the cheek.
Malcolm doesn't react; he just stares at her
without emotion.

"Oh shit," Kym whispers. "That was to-
tally inappropriate. I'm so sorry." Kym re-
treats to the front door. Tripping over her
feet. She prays he won't charge her with sexual assault. She's a big advocate for consent,
and yet, here she is fucking up.

Kym gives him one last look. He still hasn't moved or shown any kind of emotion. She says, "I'm really sorry." Then she shuts the door. Once she has caught her breath, she peeks out the window, hiding behind the lace curtains. Just like the other two women.

Malcolm is smiling and staring into nothing. Kym can hear the women chuckling. Malcolm glances at the women, straightens up, serious face on and returns to his car. Kym knows she should still feel mortified about the kiss on the cheek, but, she's enjoying his elation a little too much. 'Could he really like me?' she thinks to herself. But she also wonders if he was just laughing at her.

That answer comes to her when Kym bumps into Malcolm at the cafe in town later that very day. While she is wrapped up cosily on the comfy chair near the fire, sipping on hot chocolate with her laptop in front of her and writing a chapter for Eddie on time-travelling highlanders. It was almost something from a romantic comedy. Like what Eddie is wanting Kym to write about. She takes mental notes as the scene plays out. Malcolm approaches her, his soft smile points directly at her. He takes the seat across from her. He sits on the end and leans against his knees. His smile never drops.

"Hello," Kym says, closing her laptop and tightening her grip on the mug.

"Aye, hello," he says. "I saw ye and thought that... well..."

Kym smiles at his stammering. She finds it both cute and intriguing. 'Do I really have this kind of power over someone?' she thinks to herself.

He clears his throat and re-centres himself. He finally speaks, "There's a wee get-together tonight at the pub. Ye were wanting to get a feel for the culture. Would ye like to come along?"

Kym smiles, and the subtext of the question goes right over her head. She hasn't realised that Malcolm has asked her out. She'll find that out later. But right now, she says yes, making his smile even brighter. His skin turns a little pink at the cheeks. He gets up to return to work. Before he exits, he gives her one last look.

"I can pick ye up at six," he says.

"I could walk," she replies, once again, missing the point of the invitation.

"I'll be driving that way already, lass," he says.

Kym tries to, somewhat successfully, ignore the goosebumps she gets when Malcolm calls her 'lass.'

"No, no. I could use the exercise." This final comment from her is enough to make him give up. But he never loses that smile.

She spends the rest of the afternoon typing up the chapter for Eddie. She finds herself distracted by the thought of going out tonight. She isn't one for crowds and even contemplating calling in sick. But, she still feels guilty about kissing him on the cheek without permission. But, judging by his relaxed demeanour just then, she feels that he won't press charges after all.

Once her time-travelling chapter is

done, she writes up an email to Eddie, defending her pursuit of the time-travelling highlanders.

Hey Eddie,

I know you said no time travelling highlanders, but this guy, Malcolm, he has a few copies, and I've also caught a couple of the residents reading them.

So, I've typed up a chapter, using Laura and her new road trip in the 16th century.

Enjoy,
Kym

The sun has just gone down and Kym stands outside the pub. She can hear someone inside slurring an Elvis song. Kym takes a moment to guess that it is *Hound Dog*. That's when she spies the sign. It's Elvis karaoke night. Kym cringes and contemplates leaving. But as she looks back in the direction of the

B&B, she sees Malcolm.

He's wearing a nice cerulean coloured, button-up shirt, tucked into black slacks. He also wears a thick, dark brown jacket. She smiles at the effort he put into his hair. It is smartly styled with a slight ruffle.

Kym isn't dressed as nice. She didn't bring any nice clothes with her. Everything was about comfort to her. So tonight, she's wearing a blue tee, brown jeans and a thick green cardigan.

He smiles as he wanders over. His eyes always locked on hers. "Ye came," he says.

A little doubt fills Kym. "I thought you invited me."

"What? I did. I just... I don't know why I thought ye might not," he says. He clears his throat and gestures towards the door. "Shall we go in?"

"You didn't tell me it was Elvis Night," Kym says.

"Is that a problem?" he asks. "Sorry, I should've mentioned it."

"No, no. It's okay," she says quickly. "A little

warning would have helped. Then I could prepare for drunk, elderly men who think they can sing."

Malcolm laughs. "Dinna worry, I'll not be singing tonight."

Before going inside, Kym contemplates taking a photo and sending it to Eddie to let him know she's trying new things to write this book. She thinks 'this is a rom-com thing, right?' But, before she can take out her phone, Malcolm places his hand on the small of her back and gestures for her to go inside.

Once inside, the music hits Kym hard. As does the crowd. Kym one hundred percent... no five hundred per cent regrets her decision to come. It looks like everyone in the village is here. The chatter is loud. Kym can barely hear what Malcolm is trying to say to her.

"What?" Kym shouts.

Malcolm gets in close to her ear and says, "There's a table over there with some of ma mates."

Kym nods and follows him over to the standing table where two men were. They greet Malcolm with manly excitement and introduce themselves to Kym. The tall, slim guy with red hair was Nathan, Malcolm's colleague, and a shorter bald guy was Peter. Kym has no idea what Peter does, and frankly, she never asks.

Over the course of a few Elvis numbers, with terrible impersonation, the group have had a couple of pints each. Kym still can't hear a damn thing that they're saying. Instead, she just nods and smiles when she notices the guys trying to talk to her. She is still regretting coming tonight, but if she's honest with herself, she is enjoying Malcolm's company. Every so often they share a quick glance and a smile.

Victor, from the post office, finishes the song and the crowd cheers. Each time there's a break between the songs, Kym savours the moment that her ears aren't pounding.

"Another round?" Malcolm asks the table.

Kym assesses her glass and then gestures for half a glass this time. Like lightning Malcolm heads for the bar.

Jill, from the bookshop, in case you forgot who she is, is also the MC for the night and approaches the stage. "Thank ya for that... entertaining performance, Victor. Can someone make sure he doesn't drive home."

The crowd laughs as Victor waves her off and stumbles into his chair.

Jill continues, "Now we have the performance who we've all been waiting for. Greg." The crowd erupts into applause. Jill looks confused. "Greg? Greg!"

"He's havin a smoke," someone from the crowd yells.

"Can someone go get the bastard. Everyone has been waiting to hear his bloody song."

Kym giggles as she finishes her drink.

"Ye've made quite the impression on our lad," Peter says.

"What?" Kym asks confused.

"Usually, cannae get him out at all.," Peter says with a smile.

Kym looks over to Malcolm as he talks to the person behind the bar. She begins to panic but is able to control it at this point. She keeps her eyes focused on the empty glass.

The crowd begins clapping as Greg makes his way to the stage. "Ach, just making an entrance, lass," Greg says.

Malcolm arrives back, juggling three pints and a middy. He hands them around while looking at the stage.

"Ye'll love this one," Malcolm says to Kym. "He's why we have this every month." He takes note of Kym's concerned look. "Ye okay?"

"Looks like someone's figured it out," Nathan laughs.

Malcolm ignores Nathan and gives his full attention to Kym. "Kym? Ye alright?"

Kym throws on a fake smile. In fact, the lights are getting brighter to her. The chatter cause bugs under her skin. She says, "Everything's fine. Just feeling that last pint."

Greg starts singing on the stage. He's the only one tonight that's a dead ringer for Elvis. His song of choice: *Can't Help Falling in Love*. The crowd goes quiet to listen. A couple of the older men in the crowd initiate a dance with their partners. Kym stares. Trying to process the information she's received. 'Is tonight a date?' she thinks to herself. 'He would have said so, right?' She stares at Malcolm, who just smiles at her.

Panic has set in. Kym is taking the words of the song too literal and questions how she feels about Malcolm. The only thing that she can think of is to finally leave. Chasing the fresh air.

"I'll be back in a minute," she rattles off quickly.

Kym leaves, focusing on not trying to make a scene. Her heart is racing. While yes, she's been flirting with Malcolm, she never thought that he'd be interested in return. She figured that he was keen to be friends. 'He told me he's still getting over his wife's death,' she thinks to herself.

A gibbous moon sits above the loch, throwing silver speckles over the ripples caused by the natural fauna. The music from the pub can still be heard but it is faded, and

Greg is part way through his song.

Kym stands across the road by the loch. Soaking in the landscape and enjoying the lower amount of stimulation. She can hear someone approaching. Malcolm is walking over to her. Kym looks back out to the loch. Questioning why she didn't just leave. She normally leaves when she's uncomfortable.

"You live in such a beautiful place," Kym says.

Kym shivers a little from the sudden cool breeze. She pulls her cardigan tighter around her. Suddenly, she feels at warm blanket around her. It's Malcolm placing his jacket on her shoulders.

Kym's heart pounds and her breaths deepen. The song in the distance only adds to her anxiety. It all feels too perfect. Just like those romance books that she's been reading for research. She turns to Malcolm, wanting to talk but not knowing what to say.

Malcolm slowly moves closer to her. His eyes drop to her mouth, only for a fraction of a second. He swallows. He asks, "Can I kiss ye?"

Kym forgets to breathe. She hasn't been asked this question since her last relationship… in high school. All she manages is a single nod. Malcolm presses his mouth on hers and they share a simple tender kiss.

When the song finishes, Kym realises what they're doing and stops herself. Taking a step back from Malcolm, she holds a hand between the two. Malcolm watches her, not saying a thing.

She's unable to look him in the eye. "I'm sorry," Kym whispers.

Before Malcolm has a chance to reply, Kym walks away. Malcolm doesn't follow.

Kym walks straight back to the B&B. And when she climbs into the bed, she wants to call someone. Anyone. She needs to talk this out with someone. And it was now, at this moment, that she feels completely and utterly alone.

6

CHAPTER FOR EDDIE

TIME TRAVELLING HIGHLANDERS

I woke up from that dream again. The one with the hunk of a man, walking up the hill, eyes on me with need. I never really knew where he was from and whether his need was sexual or his desire to eat me. Literally eat me. My meat ripped from bones eating. Not the fun kind.

I dragged myself out of the now soaking wet bed and sleepily stumbled to the kitchen to not only get a drink of water but munch on a stick of butter. At this moment, I was grateful that I lived alone. I can only imagine the sight if someone was to walk in on me right now.

I was wearing my PJ bottoms that had a giant hole gaping at my left butt cheek. A singlet with ten... no thirteen moth holes. I tied up my hair for no reason at all as I'll be taking it down the moment I make it back to bed. But anyway, my hair was tied up in a mess, held together by my high school scrunchy that still smelt like my first boyfriend who was too scared to take my virginity. For some reason, I liked to remind myself of that guy.

After three mouthfuls of salted, 100% Australian butter, I felt a shiver through my body. The light of the fridge flickered. Electricity sparkled. I looked at the butter and for some reason wondered if that much fat in such a short amount of time could make me hallucinate.

"Lady Lura?" said a gruff, very masculine, deep, seductive voice.

I turned my head, stick of butter still in my hand, and looked at the intruder in my house. He was the same hunk of a man that I'd just dreamt about. He was wearing a thick, I'm assuming woollen, kilt that was dark blue with thin strips of red throughout. His dark hair was thick locks of wet lumps. His eyes were... actually, it was too dark to see his eye colour, but they did look at me with the same need. Though, this time it definitely seemed more like he wanted to eat me... in the bad way... I mean the bad-bad way, not the good-bad way.

Before I could get too excited, his stench filled the room. He smelt like he hadn't bathed in a century. It wasn't even a sweaty smell. Sweat smells nice... when hygiene is good of course. But his stench made me want to throw up the stick of butter I'd just ate.

"Ye need to come with me," the hunky, smelly, Scottish man said.

"Excuse me?" I replied with raised eyebrows.

"I've been sent from the 16th century to come and collect ye."

"Me? Why?"

"I dinnae ask why. I'm just doing what I'm asked."

"So, you always do what everyone asks?"

He reached out to me and I took a step back. That didn't seem to make him too happy, as he then took hold of me, threw me over his shoulder and carried me two steps and into the 16th century... I think... I don't know, I could be in the stone age for all I knew.

But at least I still have half a stick of the salted, 100% Australian butter. I quickly scoffed it down before I was asked to share.

The hunky, smelly, Scottish man threw me to the ground. His carelessness meant I ended up in a mud puddle. My backside was now covered in thin, slimy mud that made me smell like stale dirt.

"What the fuck!" I screamed at him.

"Get up," he said as he pulled me from the mud puddle in a single move.

I tried to struggle free from him, but his bone-crushing grip was beyond me. That is until I remembered his member. I drove my knee into his family jewels. I was worried that thick kilt would pad him, but he released me and gave out a cry. I took that moment of freedom to leg it out of there. I was pretty surprised that I was a lot faster than him. Maybe the fact that he was weighed down with that woollen kilt and crying in pain is why I had an advantage.

I wish I could say my escape was an elegant and majestic getaway, but I fell several times, covering myself with not only mud but grass and what I can only hope was berries.

I ran through a forest and stumbled into a secret stone area. A sparkling pond was surrounded by mossy rocks. On the other side of that pond, a very attractive man stood watching me. He had red scruffy hair and a surprisingly well-trimmed beard. Over his muscular chest he wore a light brown tunic and to compliment that, he wore a kilt the same colour as hunky, smelly, Scottish man.

I was just about to dub this guy Handsome, Red, Scottish Man, but he then said with the sweetest, masculine voice I'd ever heard, "Ma name is Dunmor." His eyes went over my shoulder. "I apologise for Angus' behaviour. He was just meant to collect ye."

I flung around to see Hunky, Smelly, Scottish Man standing there. I picked up a rock and threw it at him. As I backed away from him, I threw rocks at him. And I'm afraid to admit, sometimes I threw leaves.

"Lady Laura," Dunmor, the handsome, red, Scotsman, said, "we're not gonna harm ye."

"Yeah sure, kidnap me from my home, bring me here, throw me in mud, then chase me. Sure, trust the time-travelling highlanders."

"Angus, leave us," Dunmor said.

The smelly Angus grunts then exited this little stone area. My attention went to Dunmor. His curious gaze on me.

"What?" I snapped. "Why am I here?"

"The fates have determined we are to marry," he said so straight-faced I laughed.

"Nice one."

"I'll tell ye the truth, Lady Laura. The fates have explained that ye're the only woman I'm meant to marry."

"What? You can't find someone in your time?" I couldn't help but start laughing again. I leaned up against one of the large stones and shook my head at him.

"We are to marry by the end of the day," he said.

"Not bloody likely."

"I have brought ye appropriate wear to change into. Your current attire is not acceptable."

I clench my teeth, almost biting my tongue off. "Are you listening to me? It's not happening."

He threw a bundle of clothes at my feet. Now, I didn't want to follow his directions, I mean, I didn't want to give him any false hope. For all I knew, by wearing these clothes I could be agreeing to staying with him for eternity. But, as I shivered in the cold, those dry woollen fabrics were way too tempting.

"Turn around," I barked. "We're not married, so you don't get to see all this." I pointed at my body, then spun my finger at him. Once he turned, I untied the bundle.

I pulled out a dress, full-body undergarments and a thick woven shawl, the same colour as his kilt. There was no way on this planet, in any time period, that the dress and undergarments would fit.

"Wow, are you serious? This shit would never fit me." I chucked the dress and undergarments towards him. Sadly, it only travelled about a metre before hitting the ground, making the dramatic moment moot. "What? You think I was going to be a petite woman. I'm proud of my height, lazy lifestyle and these curves."

"You are indeed a healthy choice," he said.

"Healthy choice?" I growled.

I wrapped the shawl around me, for protection against the cold and left the small stone area. Sadly, Angus was waiting just outside. I returned to Dunmor and said, "You do realise kidnapping someone to marry them is frowned upon."

"Not when the fates have determined our marriage."

"Oh my god. Make life choices of your own, you drongo," I growled. "Let me talk to them?"

He curled his brows. "Who?"

"The fates. I want to hear it from the fates

themselves."

"Only Kerrigan can speak to them," he said.

"Well, take me to Kerrigan."

"We don't have any horses. She's at least a four-day journey."

"Well, you should have thought of that before bringing me here."

"But this is a sacred place. This is the ideal place to marry."

"We are not getting married. Take me to Kargan."

"Kerrigan."

"Whatever."

I eventually won my argument, and we began the treacherous journey to what Dunmor called the Druid of Karrigan. Which was a weird name, seeming that her first name was Karrigan, meaning she was the druid of herself.

But alas, I found myself on another road trip. Though, I'm not really sure I could call this a road trip. We only used roads sometimes. Maybe more of a hiking trip. I was still getting over the last one. Where I definitely did not have a thing for anyone of the other characters... I mean, people who I met along the way.

There were absolutely no feelings towards Billy, Scott or Davey. And there was especially nothing going on between me and Davey. Anyone who thinks so is wrong. I may have had a thing for Steve, but not anyone else.

7

SWIVEL

Kym bites into the toast and regrets the action immediately. She doesn't feel like toast after all. Hoping tea would help, she tries that. But no success. A moment of depression consumes her. She feels alone and stuck. Work is relying on her to write something, but the mere thought of writing makes her as uncomfortable as eating the toast.

Especially a stupid romance that her stupid publishers want.

It has been a few days since Kym kissed Malcolm. Neither had contacted each other. She hasn't even left the B&B. So, it can't really be his fault for not contacting her? But it can't be her fault either. Right?

Kym wonders if this is some kind of normal romance trope. The awkward standoff between the leading man and woman. A moment of miscommunication. She wonders if Eddie would find that too tropey. She scribbles down a note to ask Eddie is she can add it to the stupid romance that her stupid publishers want.

Kym looks at her laptop. The words Chapter Two are mocking her. She isn't sure where to take this new time travel story that's just a sequel to *Autumn's Spring*. But since she hasn't heard from Eddie, the chapter must be okay, now that it's hitting those romance cliches. Even though it makes her cringe while writing such... genres, she knows she'll push through in order to meet her contract obligations.

"Stupid romance. Stupid Publishers," she mumbles to herself.

But right now, she can do nothing but stare at the screen while thinking about the other night with Malcolm. She cringes at the memory of the Elvis impersonator singing in the background. Then shifts to goosebumps as she remembered the cold, crisp air that led to Malcolm's jacket around her shoulders. The...

Kym slaps herself to get away from the memory. She shouldn't be thinking about this. She has a book to write. A book about time-travelling highlanders. She definitely shouldn't be thinking about the Scottish police officer who kept her warm as he...

A tap at the door steals her attention. Her heart races. She fears it's Malcolm, coming to say Malcolm things and win her over. She doesn't want that. Or does she?

Another tap at the door.

Kym tidies herself up and swaps out the robe with a long jacket. She wants to look a little presentable if Malcolm is at the door.

Wait... What? She shouldn't be thinking that. But she is.

Kym kinda reluctantly finally opens the door.

"Eddie," she gasps. "What? Why? Uh... Were the chapters that bad?"

"Yeah, they were that bad," he says with a smile. "I said no time-travelling highlanders."

"So you got on a plane?" she says. She leaves him at the front door, expecting him to follow. He does. "Feel free to have some toast and I'll make some more tea."

He sits down at the table and indeed takes a piece of toast from Kym's plate.

"No coffee?" he calls as he covers his mouth to avoid spitting crumbs everywhere.

"I ran out of coffee," Kym says as she puts the kettle on. "But I can get some from Maggie."

"No, no. It's okay. I'll survive with tea."

She takes her time with making the tea. It was thoughts of how angry Eddie might be that kept her distracted. It was originally worry but quickly turned into frustration. Damn it, she knew that time-traveling highlanders sell. Kym wonders why he won't let her write one. Does he want her to fail, she thinks as she slams the tea and cup on the table.

"So, what? Are you staying here then?" Kym bluntly as she sat in her chair.

"I'm sensing some strong feelings with the fact that I'm here."

"Why are you here?"

"Didn't we just discuss this?" Eddie says. "I just travelled half the globe to make sure you're okay."

"Do you want a medal?" Kym says with eyes rolling.

"Hey, what's up? What's going on?"

"I don't know," Kym whines then puts her head on the table.

"Maybe you coming here was a bad idea. I'm sorry. I thought a change of scenery might help."

"It did... Until it didn't... And it kinda still does, but it also doesn't."

Kym is starting to feel an itching sensation around her body. She taps her forehead on the table a few times before pouting at Eddie.

Eddie raises his eyebrows. "Shall we go home?"

Kym's heart struggles a little. She doesn't know if she wants to or not. She feels there's nothing waiting for her at home. But she wonders if there might actually be something here. Kym once again puts her forehead against the table.

"Look," Eddie starts, "I don't know what's going on exactly, but these chapters you sent me... they're not you. Which tells me something serious must be happening. Because even when you were in the ICU in hospital that week, you still wrote amazing stuff."

Kym looks up at Eddie. His worried eyes on hers. In this light, 'he looks kinda cute' she thinks. She immediately sits up straight.

"There's something wrong with me," she admits.

"I know that," he says. "Which is why I'm here to help."

"I think I'm feeling that romance stuff people go on about."

Eddie laughs. "Romance stuff? You mean you like someone?"

"I think so," she says. "And I don't like it. It feels... confusing."

"Who's the lucky person?"

"He's a local police officer, Malcolm," she says.

Kym finds she can't stay still while her

thoughts are on Malcolm. So she fills the teapot back up.

"Wait, he's the one that reads about time-traveling highlanders?"

"Yup," she says, not even wanting to go further into Malcolm's devastating history and why he owned such romance novels.

Eddie stares at his tea, tapping his finger against the porcelain handle. "A cop, hey," he says.

"Have you done something illegal?" Kym says.

"What? No. Why would you ask something like that?"

"Well, you looked super awkward the moment I mentioned he was a cop."

"It has nothing to do with that," he says. He finally gives her his attention. "So, any chance you can try another chapter? One that isn't about time-travellers."

"But it was a sequel, like you said, and I followed some tropes."

"No time-travelling highlanders," he scowls. "I mean it."

"I myea myit," she mimics teasingly.

"Mock me all you want, I'm vetoing it," he says, leaning back and folding his arms.

Kym pokes her tongue at Eddie, which he was quite happy to return the gesture.

"Look, if dating this cop will give you some inspiration you should do it."

"What?"

"What? You said you don't know much about the romancey stuff, and you said you might be feeling that romancey stuff at the moment. Use it to write a story. Scottish villages are a trope that sells well."

"But Eddie, I just told you I'm confused about it."

"Well, only one way to not be confused and that's to dive in and suss it out."

"Why don't you dive in and suss it out," she whines.

"Because I'm not the one writing a book," he says with a raised eyebrow. He takes a sip of the tea and spits it back into the cup. "What the hell is this?"

"Earl Grey," Kym says with an evil smirk.

He puts the cup down and pushes it away. "Maybe I'll have some coffee. You said it was with Maggie? I'll go get some."

"Or, we can go to the local cafe. You'll love it," she says, then spies the time. "Though, Malcolm does go there around this time. It might be awkward."

"Why awkward?" he asks, propping his chin on his hand and arching an eyebrow. "What did you do?"

Her gaze starts to shift around the room and she picks at the toast on her plate.

"Oh, well, you see, we kinda went on this date, that I didn't know was a date, and then we kinda, you know, kissed a little, then I ran back here... and we haven't really spoken since."

She finally looks at him. His face was blank until he stifled a laugh. He shook his head a little.

"Don't laugh at me," she snaps.

"Not laughing at you. I'm laughing with you," he says.

"Do you see me laughing?"

"You are on the inside," he says, once again reading her mind, as she was in fact, laughing inside. "Come on, I want to go see the guy who has captured my favourite writer's attention."

"Well, buddy, take some notes because I'm going to nail this romancey stuff for your silly romance book."

As they walk to the café, and banter like high school kids, Kym can't help but wonder if Eddie is curious to see her crash and burn. She knows he isn't the type to want to see her fail. But Kym can't help but think about that possibility. Especially since he came all this way because of two failed chapters. She pushes the thoughts away… for now.

It's a somewhat sunny day, meaning that the two of them sit outside, sipping their coffee, and sharing a slice of double choc fudge cake. They trade stories about their most cringe-worthy teenage moments, each tale more mortifying than the last. That is until Kym spies Malcolm coming around the corner.

Malcolm glances at Kym, then at Eddie, then back to Kym. His eyes drop to the shared slice of double choc fudge cake.

"Hey, Malcolm," Kym says as she stands. "Can we talk."

With the biggest sigh Kym has ever witnessed, Malcolm approaches. He stands on the other side of the barrier. His eyes glancing to Eddie every now and then.

"Hey, sorry I haven't contacted you," Kym says. "But you should also be sorry for not contacting me." Malcolm raises an eyebrow at her. "Okay... It is true that I ran away from you, so I should probably explain why I did. But I need to say it has nothing to do with you." He breaks eye contact and looks away from her. "Okay, I'm really sorry that I ran off after we kissed and didn't contact you to tell you that I freaked out. But, I mean, when I think about it, clearly, I was upset, so you..."

Eddie interrupts Kym's rambling, "Hi, I'm Eddie. Kym's Editor."

Malcolm's gaze flicks to Eddie. "Malcolm," he finally says. "Just in?"

"This morning," Eddie says.

"Always travel this far for yer writers?" Malcolm says, surprising both Kym and Eddie.

"Only when that writer sends really bad chapters," Eddies replies and chuckles.

Eddie is trying to diffuse Malcolm's apparent standoffish demeanour through some jokes. But Malcolm kept a straight face. Kym can't help but think about this being one of those romance tropes.

"I need to get back to work," Malcolm says.

"Can we just chat for a second?" Kym asks. She then turns to Eddie. "Can you give us a second?"

"Sure. I'll go lurk in the corner and take some notes," Eddie says, then finishes his coffee. "My other authors have sent me chapters I need to read."

Kym narrows her eyes on Eddie, which he returns right back to her with a slight smirk. After a quick assessment of his belongings, Eddie takes a seat inside the café, near a window, so he can take notes for Kym. Despite the fact, that Kym was joking. Well, kinda joking. Actually, Kym needed all the help she could get.

"So, do you want to have lunch together?" Kym asks.

"I've already eaten."

"Come on, Malcolm. I'm sorry. Let's talk, please. I like you. I don't want you to hate me because I freaked out."

He releases a hard breath. "I dinnae hate ye."

"Then at least have a coffee with me... I mean tea."

"Okay. I can spare some time," he says as he takes his hat off and joins her at the table.

Ginnie comes and takes their order, her smug grin tells Kym that she must know about the kiss. Actually, the more Kym thinks about it, the more she realises that everyone in the town must know, and they must also know that she ran off. Abandoning Malcolm.

Embarrassing him.

"So, I do like you," Kym says. "It's just... it's been a while since... I've had a relationship, and that really can't be considered a relationship... I think. But, yeah, I'm like, not good with romance and stuff. In fact, it kinda weirds me out. I mean, don't get me wrong, I'm attracted to you, I just feel weird with the whole will they won't they or the whole I'm gonna try and impress, which means I'm not really going to be myself. And then there's the wining and dining, I think it's just weird. I mean, can't people just sit at home on the couch, in their PJs munching on some Ben and Jerry's..."

Kym stops talking when she notices Malcolm's massive smile. He leans forward onto the table and takes Kym's hand into his.

"Never seen ye this nervous before."

"I'm not nervous. Why would I be nervous? Okay... I'm a little... A lot nervous. I've never done this before, and by this I mean talk about my feelings... Okay, I did do the feelings thing once, like I said, but it was so long ago that I barely remember what happened. I mean, if we, you know, take things further, I just need you to be, you know, patient." Kym pauses to catch her breath. She barely notices Malcolm stroking her hand with his thumb. "So, you know, after how I treated you, after that kiss, which was a great kiss by the way, I can see why you probably don't want to, you know, go for a drink sometime... Well, another time, cause technically we're having a drink right now... Are you laughing at me?"

"Take a breath," he says, enclosing her hands in his. "I was shocked when ye left. Thought maybe I'd moved too fast. Should've checked on ye, but I wanted to give ye space."

"So, not angry with me?"

"Nae."

"And you still like me?"

"Aye, very much."

"Well... Cool."

He snorts. "Cool?" He sits back and enjoys his tea. "There's one problem."

"What's that?"

"Ye're here for, what? Another month?"

"Or two."

"Even if it's two," he pauses to glance at Eddie, who is now distracted on a call. "I could fall for ye, Kym. What happens when ye leave?"

Kym considers who Eddie is talking to; it's after hours in Perth. She wonders, 'does he speak with all his writers that late at night?' She never once considers it could be family, because that would make sense.

Woops. Back to Malcolm.

"I honestly didn't think that far ahead." Kym was so caught up in 'experiment mode' that she didn't even think about what would happen when the time came. What if she started liking him a lot? It would hurt way more than it does right now. How could she start this experiment when real feelings are involved? 'Stupid, Eddie. Tricking me with talks of research and experiments,' she thinks to herself.

Malcolm snorts again. "Maybe we should

talk about that first."

"What? Whether a two-month relationship is worth it?"

"Or, if things go well, do we, ye know... Do we stick it out?" Malcolm begins tapping his knee while bouncing the ball of his left foot.

"Long distance?"

"Or ye could stay?" he says. "I mean, I'd come to ye, but I figured it's easier for ye to move with your profession than it is with mine."

"Valid point," Kym says. She looks around the quaint little village. It was quiet. Peaceful. She could see herself staying in a place like this. "I mean, we could try it. Though, can we go slow?"

"How slow? We only have two months."

"Well... The romancey stuff I'd like to go slow with, but you know we could... I mean, I hate to suggest it, but it's also the fastest way to know."

"What's that?"

"We could, I don't know, house share.

Then we can go slow on the other stuff while seeing if we can live under the same roof."

Malcolm smiles. "Going fast while going slow."

"I mean, if we do end up wanting to stick it out, there's gonna be a crap tonne of government paperwork to do. So, pros and cons to sticking it out."

Malcolm laughs. "Sure, why not? And, seeing as time is precious, when would you like to move into the guest room?"

"Well, we could just do it today, get it out of the way."

"Sure."

Only then does she look back to see Eddie still on the phone, and as Malcolm's eyes follow hers, he sighs softly.

8
DARK MOMENT

Kym knows she has to tell Eddie the news, after all, she was sure he'd figure out she wasn't living in Australia anymore. Though, she does contemplate doing a challenge and seeing how long it would take him to realise those video calls were actually international and not down the street.

She waits until they are back in the B&B and keeps it quick when telling him. So much so that she's unsure if the words came out correctly. He just stares at her. Blinks. Stares. Blinks. Shakes his head.

"What?" he says.

"Malcolm has asked me to stay here, with him," she explains.

"And you told him he's crazy, right?"

She immediately avoids eye contact. Clearly, Eddie isn't taking this news well. She realises she should have gone with her plan to see how long until he notices. She collects her bag and opens it on the bed.

"What the hell are you doing?" Eddie's focused gaze follows Kym as she packs her bag. "You've known the man for barely three weeks."

"Well, I ain't getting any younger."

"Are you serious right now?" Disbelief rules Eddie's expression. He stands there, motionless, blinking.

Kym looks through the bedside tables for anything she may have left. Like any jellybeans that escaped the packet the other night. Sadly, she finds none.

"Kym, you can't move in with a guy you've just met."

"He's a cop, so he has to be trustworthy. And I've got nothing to go back to."

Eddie's expression shifts a little. Going a little pale, eyes low, chewing lips. He finally says, "That's not true. You have a job. People who care about you. Besides, you never believed in that romance stuff. Why now?"

"I don't know, maybe I just needed someone to take interest in me," she says. She zips up her bag and drops it on the floor, pulling up the handle. "Look, you're the one who told me to go for it."

"I said date the guy, not move in with him."

"Eddie, I'm still going to finish the book. I'm just not going back."

"You still have the book tour," he says with the flattest tone that Kym has ever heard.

"I'll come back for that."

"Are you sure he'll let you?" Again, with the super flat tone.

"Come on, he's not possessive. Look, I've already had this conversation with him. We'll try it out for a month or so, then check in to see how we're feeling."

"Kym, I need you to listen to me," Eddie says with a lick of flame. "You should not do this. At least get to know him first. Online date for a while. Just... come home, then see how you feel."

"Eddie, why do you care so much? This

doesn't affect you," she says, almost defeated by the pointless argument. She has made her decision and just wants to try out this new adventure.

Eddie doesn't speak. He doesn't even look at her. He stares off into the distance, and she wonders if his eyes are actually swelling red, or if it's just a trick of the light. He clears his throat and leaves the room.

'Typical,' she thinks to herself. She had hoped that their final conversation could be a pleasant one. She hopes that they will make up before he heads home. Knowing he needs some space, she leaves him alone and heads for the car outside. Malcolm was waiting for her with a smile.

She knew she was making the right decision... right. 'This is what normal people do,' she thinks to herself. She always wanted to be normal. And here was someone offering her normal. Maybe they were moving fast, but she was in her 30s, he was in his 40s, and they both just want to start a new chapter in their lives.

As she throws her bag into his boot, she glances back to the B&B and spies Eddie for a moment, then he slips into the shadows. She has no idea why, but something in her chest hurt. That something radiated around her body. She wonders if she just randomly needs to run. Though she was unsure of the direction, so instead, she stood still.

"Are ye okay?" Malcolm asks.

"Yup," she says. She treats that weird feeling as a weird anomaly and gets into Malcolm's car.

"So, how did Eddie take the news?" Malcolm asks.

"He thinks we're crazy," she says, placing a hand on his.

"Maybe we are." His smile brightens her mood. He slips on his sunnies, starts the car and heads to his home.

9

JOYFUL DEFEAT

Kym wakes up in Malcolm's guest room. She's a little disoriented as she sits up and looks around the room. For a moment, she thinks she's at her home in Australia, but the shapes in the shadows don't look right. As her eyes adjust, she notices the floral display that Malcolm had put up yesterday.

For the first time since arriving in Scotland, she feels uneasy. She doesn't recognise the deep hollow in her chest. It's growing fast, spreading throughout her limbs.

It surprises her that she immediately thinks of Eddie and not the hot police officer in the next room. No, he was the second thought, only to compare against Eddie. She thinks it has to do with the fact that he'll be boarding a flight sometime in the next couple of days, and she might never see him again. Yes, they may talk on the phone, or via video call, but it's never the same.

Now that she is wide awake, she feels a strong spark of inspiration. She knows exactly the kind of book she needs to write. For once, she understands the type of book that Eddie is chasing. She pulls out her laptop and searches 'how to write a romance.' Yes, it did take her this long to look up this simple question. She'd been so stubborn and so headstrong to avoid writing a romance that she didn't even bother to do a simple search on the internet.

She buys the first book that comes up, in digital of course, and she spends the next hour taking notes and sets out her chapters to be named after each of the beats. She knows immediately the story she will tell. A writer who is clueless about romance is asked to write a romance. Yes, she is one hundred per cent going to write the events of the last few weeks. Obviously, changing the names of everyone involved. Maybe even remove the names of the locations and set it in a completely different country. She figures she should also change the profession of the local that the main character declares they'll move in with.

A part of her doesn't care if it's wrong to write about her current experience. She thinks a part of this has more to do with getting Eddie to understand her motives for wanting to stay.

It's an interesting thing, writing about real events and having to get into the mind of other characters. This means that she has to get into the minds of the characters she's just named Eddie and Malcolm. She finds she has difficulty understanding Malcolm's motivations beyond doubt. Why does this character want Kym to stay? Are they that lonely? Are they the white knight that Kym thought she desperately needed, and he just needs to rescue someone? Was he a part of a cult that requires a sacrifice of a woman who chooses to leave her home on a whim? 'Any are plausible,' she thinks to herself.

But with Eddie's character, she immediately knows his motivation. He's worried about her. He sees someone he cares about making a drastic decision so suddenly. He comes to Scotland to see if she's okay. He can tell her state of mental health through her creative works. And these last chapters... he knows something is wrong and he knows that a phone call isn't the amount of helps she needs. She needs someone beside her, telling her with no hesitation that she was making a very bad choice. Or at the very least, tells her to give it more time to make the choice.

It takes two days of solid writing for Kym to make it to the end of the manuscript. Her first draft is done. Malcolm gives her the space she needs to write. It was something she's grateful for. He completely understood what she needs when it came to writing. But Eddie... Eddie knows what she needs as a person. He's always looking out for her career and her wellbeing. 'But his career does rely on her work,' she thinks as doubt consumes her momentarily.

She sits back in the chair, laptop on her lap, staring out Malcolm's lounge window watching the snowfall. She always thought Eddie was just her editor, but he is... 'Is he, my friend?' Kym wonders to herself.

"Wait... Do I actually have a friend?" she says out loud.

This realisation hits her hard. She has never really had a friend before, so this is a strange feeling for her. She has family, a rather bad family, which is why she never thinks about them. So, there's negative con-notation there. Which is why she never really invested into relationships. Which has her wondering, why she would truly stay here. 'Am I running away?' she asks herself.

She looks at the clock. It's nearly midday. If she goes to the B&B now, she might just see Eddie before he leaves.

Without putting decent clothes on, Kym shrugs on a long jacket, buttons it up, slips on some boots, pops her laptop into her satchel, around the shoulder it goes, and she finally dashes out the door. Malcolm was out, so she doesn't have a car she can use. So, in true rom-com fashion, she makes a run for it.

Kym manages to make it to the letterbox before she keels over in pain and agony. Sucking in breaths, she stands up and this time chooses to walk. The triumphant mad run to her best friend is now a limping walk. But at least her heart and intentions are still the same.

Kym arrives at the B&B. She stands outside, a little elated, a little terrified, and a little thankful that she finally understands. She takes a deep breath, opens the door, walks right in, and as she starts to climb those stairs Maggie calls after her, "If you're looking for your friend, he left early this morning."

Kym pauses on the fifth step. She stares towards the top off the stairs. She grips the hard wood handrail so tight that she imagines a hairline crack running down the length of the staircase. She knows she needs to breathe but the air tastes too stale.

"He left very quietly. I think his plane is leaving sometime around now. Apparently, he managed to get an earlier flight. I guess he didn't want to stay around after you and

Malcolm moved in together. Can I just say how sweet it is to see, I mean you've only known..." Maggie doesn't stop talking, but Kym switches off.

'This isn't what happens in those rom-coms,' she thinks to herself. She considers writing in the book version that she catches Eddie, and they have a long happy conversation. Where they make up and declare their friendship with one another. Maybe even hug it out. But Kym knows she shouldn't, because she thinks a part of her knows there is more to the end of the story. She cannot just hug it out. Maybe her major declaration isn't running to meet him at the airport, but instead, finish writing this romance book and email it to him.

"Do you mind if I use your dining area to send him an email?" Kym asks. Her eyes don't quite meet Maggie's.

"Of course, Hun," Maggie says. "I'll make you some tea."

Kym pulls herself to the dining room and sits at the small table that she'd been eating at for the last three weeks. She opens her laptop, writes in the last chapter what has happened in the last couple of hours, where she attempted to meet Eddie. Missing him, then writing this last attempt to let him understand her choice and how she doesn't want to lose her only friend. That she is contemplating returning but doesn't know what the best option is for her. After all, she is trying to chase normal.

SEND EMAIL

CLICK